Charles Busch's
Cleopatra

A Samuel French Acting Edition

SAMUEL
FRENCH
FOUNDED 1830

SAMUELFRENCH.COM
SAMUELFRENCH-LONDON.CO.UK

FOR PRODUCTION ENQUIRIES

UNITED STATES AND CANADA
Info@SamuelFrench.com
1-866-598-8449

UNITED KINGDOM AND EUROPE
Plays@SamuelFrench-London.co.uk
020-7255-4302

Each title is subject to availability from Samuel French, depending upon country of performance. Please be aware that CHARLES BUSCH'S CLEOPATRA may not be licensed by Samuel French in your territory. Professional and amateur producers should contact the nearest Samuel French office or licensing partner to verify availability.

MUSIC USE NOTE

Licensees are solely responsible for obtaining formal written permission from copyright owners to use copyrighted music in the performance of this play and are strongly cautioned to do so. If no such permission is obtained by the licensee, then the licensee must use only original music that the licensee owns and controls. Licensees are solely responsible and liable for all music clearances and shall indemnify the copyright owners of the play(s) and their licensing agent, Samuel French, against any costs, expenses, losses and liabilities arising from the use of music by licensees. Please contact the appropriate music licensing authority in your territory for the rights to any incidental music.

IMPORTANT BILLING AND CREDIT REQUIREMENTS

If you have obtained performance rights to this title, please refer to your licensing agreement for important billing and credit requirements.

CHARLES BUSCH'S CLEOPATRA was first produced by the Theatre for the New City (Crystal Field, Executive Artistic Director) in New York City on March 25, 2016.The performance was directed by Carl Andress, with sets and grpahics by B.T. Whitehill, costumes by Jessica Jahn, lights by Zach Blane, sound by Bart Fasbender, and wigs by Katherine Carr. The cast was as follows:

CLEOPATRA	Charles Busch
CAESAR/CALPURNIA/LEDIPUS	Tony Sheldon
MARK ANTONY	Joe Zaso
OCTAVIAN/OCTAVIA	Jennifer Van Dyck
CHARMION	Ashley Austin Morris
IRAS	Jennifer Cody
SOOTHSAYER	Andy Halliday
APOLLODORUS/ACHMED	Larry Bullock

CHARACTERS

CLEOPATRA – Legendary Queen of the Nile. Beautiful, tough and alluring.

CAESAR – Magnetic Roman leader in his late middle age.

MARK ANTONY – Handsome, gruff warrior with a fatal weakness for women.

OCTAVIAN – Young, ruthlessly ambitious heir to Caesar.

APOLLODORUS – Musclebound devoted slave to Cleopatra.

SOOTHSAYER – Nervous, highly emotional wandering prophet.

CHARMION – Beautiful young handmaiden to Cleopatra and very much in charge/

IRAS – Lovely handmaiden to Cleopatra, with a bawdy sense of humor

CALPURNIA – Caesar's imposing and imperious wife.

OCTAVIA – Octavian's gentle and delicately beautiful twin sister.

LEPIDUS – A worldly and dignified elder Roman Senator.

ACHMED – A violent, unscrupulous slave trader.

CASTING NOTE

The original production had a cast of eight actors, with several roles doubled. The play can also be performed with a larger cast each playing only one role.

Several roles in the original production used cross gender casting. This is not a necessity. What is important is that each role be played with total conviction. The humor must not derive from the role being played by someone of the opposite sex, but from the lines and situation being comic.

Suggested doubling and gender crossed casting
Octavian/ Octavia… played by a woman
Caesar/ Calpurnia/ Lepidus…played by a man
Apollodorus/ Achmed…played by a man
Cleopatra… played by a man

Scene One

(CAESAR and MARK ANTONY enter. The actor playing ANTONY announces "A camp near Tarsus!" The lights shift and we are in the scene.)

ANTONY. Personally, Caesar, if it was up to me, Egypt would be a Roman state. I'd teach these Cobra worshipping mystics the way of the world with my bare fists and the lash.

CAESAR. Mark Antony, I pray in time that a wise head shall be placed upon that glorious torso. It is in Rome's best interests to make Egypt a grateful ally rather than a bitter conquest.

ANTONY. Forgive my brutish ways. I've spent too many years sweating and grunting among men in battle.

(YOUNG OCTAVIAN enters.)

OCTAVIAN. Great Uncle, there you are. I searched for you throughout this military encampment. And here I find you in a billet barely suitable for a foot soldier.

CAESAR. Octavian, your young eyes have been dazzled by the grandeur you've observed on your travels.

OCTAVIAN. What an education you have provided for me. With Father dying so unexpectedly and Mother being, well, *Mother*, the man I am today is what you have made of me.

CAESAR. And we're still working on it. You are acquainted with the Tribune Mark Antony?

ANTONY. An honor, young Gaius Octavius.

OCTAVIAN. We met once before, Tribune. Years ago when I was a lad of twelve you escorted Mother and me to a chariot race at the coliseum. I sat beside you and had the privilege of wiping your dripping brow.

ANTONY. It was murderously hot that day.

OCTAVIAN. No, it was unseasonably frigid. *Mother* has a way of making even the most cool headed perspire. Great Uncle, do you know your military encampment is replete with a wild-eyed Soothsayer?

CAESAR. Well, that's what makes it camp.

OCTAVIAN. This Soothsayer claims to have prophecies for both you and for Queen Cleopatra of Egypt.

ANTONY. He won't find the Egyptian wench here.

CAESAR. That is cause for celebration. It is my unpleasant task to choose an Egyptian ruler among embattled royal siblings who believe they are descended from wild beasts of prey.

OCTAVIAN. I trust you've arrived at a conclusion.

CAESAR. I have. Rome will be in support of young King Ptolemy. Can't say I'm terribly impressed with the lad. Generations of inbreeding have given him crossed eyes and a most unpleasant sneer.

ANTONY. A decadent wastrel. Oh, yeah, I can just see the boy Pharaoh bent over a sarcophagus with his royal retinue taking turns boffing him in his hairless Egyptian ass.

OCTAVIAN. *(Trying to focus despite his attraction to* **ANTONY.***)* Pray, Uncle, what made you side against his sister Cleopatra?

CAESAR. She is nowhere to be found. It is said that she has fled to Syria. An odd way to fight for a crown.

OCTAVIAN. Perhaps she was "assisted" in her flight.

CAESAR. Are you saying that her brothers' advisors may have *reunited* the Queen with her ancestors?

ANTONY. It is also said that the young Queen is a creature of the rarest beauty.

CAESAR. Well, her beauty is one for the ages. We can only assume that she is dead and her remains blown through the desert winds.

(**APOLLODORUS** *enters carrying a large rolled up rug.*)

APOLLODORUS. A rug of Persia. A gift for Caesar from Nayan the merchant.

CAESAR. *(Impatiently.)* Yes, yes, put it down, man, and go. We have business here.

ANTONY. *(Suspicious.)* Tradesman, would it not be easier to sling the rug over your shoulder?

APOLLODORUS. Not a rug of this rare quality.

(**APOLLODORUS** *gently places it on the ground.*)

CAESAR. Antony, lend me your sword. This rug may require some cutting.

APOLLODORUS. *(Alarmed.)* Cutting?

(**ANTONY** *gives* **CAESAR** *his sword.*)

APOLLODORUS. Please don't. The rug is such a delicate weave.

CAESAR. We shall see about that.

(*Before* **CAESAR** *can violently plunge his sword into the rug,* **APOLLODORUS** *unrolls it and lo and behold inside is the ravishing young* **CLEOPATRA**.)

APOLLODORUS. All hail Cleopatra! Kindred of Ra, beloved of the moon and sun, and of Upper and Lower Egypt, Queen.

CLEOPATRA. Greetings, Caesar, from Egypt.

CAESAR. Most amusing. But I am far too busy for levity. Merchant, take away the rug and your young charge.

(**APOLLODORUS** *throws the rug over his shoulder.*)

CLEOPATRA. But hey! Wait just a minute. Dontcha recognize my face from the coin?

CAESAR. No. Can't say I do. Away with you.

CLEOPATRA. I am Queen I tell you. I have the royal beauty mark behind my ear to prove it.

(**ANTONY** *looks behind her ear.*)

ANTONY. She's got it.

CAESAR. But why are you so much fairer than all others on your dark continent?

CLEOPATRA. Well, it might be on account of my second cousin on my mother's side being a white leopard.

OCTAVIAN. It takes more to be a Cleopatra than a pale complexion and a beauty mark. Come, girl.

> (ANTONY *and* OCTAVIAN *reach for her arms. She shakes them both off.*)

CLEOPATRA. Great Caesar, you gotta listen. I am Cleopatra. My brother had me abducted me to the desert and left there to die. My loyal servant Apollodorus with great daring brought me all the way here for your protection.

ANTONY. (*Looking at* APOLLODORUS.) *She* saved you from death? Ha! Don't make me laugh.

CLEOPATRA. How dare you!

> (*She springs at him like a tigress. He grabs her wrists.*)

ANTONY. Wildcat! Hellion!

CLEOPATRA. Nobody insults Apollodorus. And I'm the only one allowed to call her "she."

CAESAR. Antony, under the circumstances, I believe you owe the fellow an apology.

ANTONY. (*Begrudgingly.*) If you insist, Great Caesar, then… I apologize.

APOLLODORUS. I accept.

> (*He winks at* ANTONY *lasciviously.*)

CLEOPATRA. You may leave us. Wait for me without.

APOLLODORUS. As you wish, Mistress.

CLEOPATRA. Thanks, Doris.

> (APOLLODORUS *exits.*)

CAESAR. I must inform you, Cleopatra of Egypt, that in your absence I have forged an alliance with your brother, Ptolemy.

CLEOPATRA. Don't trust him for a minute. My father wished upon his death that I be crowned Queen of the Nile. He had to throw in my brother as part of the deal. Lo and behold, my husband had me kidnapped in dead of night.

CAESAR. Your husband? I thought you said your brother had you kidnapped.

CLEOPATRA. I meant my brother.

CAESAR. But you clearly said your husband.

CLEOPATRA. I meant my husband.

CAESAR. But first you said your brother. Don't lie to me, child! Who was it?!

CLEOPATRA. He's my brother and my husband! That's how we royals do things in Egypt. We were married four years ago. Some wedding. The day every girl dreams about. You walk down the aisle and who's waiting for you but your crazy kid brother. *(She starts to sob.)*

CAESAR. Get ahold of yourself, child.

CLEOPATRA. I can't.

OCTAVIAN. Tears are not becoming for one with claims to a throne.

ANTONY. With your permission, Caesar, I must return to my legion. Gaius Octavius, you may join me.

OCTAVIAN. That would be an honor. Farewell, Great Uncle.

(**ANTONY** *and* **OCTAVIAN** *turn to leave.*)

CLEOPATRA. *(Imperiously.)* I haven't dismissed you yet!

OCTAVIAN. The child has the arrogance of a Queen if not the footwear.

(**CLEOPATRA** *checks her shoes.*)

(They exit.)

CLEOPATRA. I hate them. I hope they are stricken with the plague. I hope they get run over by a team of horses. I hope they…

CAESAR. Come, child, sit on my lap.

CLEOPATRA. Okay.

> *(She sits on his lap. Still whimpering. He dips into a bowl and takes out a delicacy.)*

CAESAR. Here, have a piece of dried chuba root. It's a delicacy. You'll like it.

CLEOPATRA. Never had chuba before. I'm scared. Maybe it's poisoned.

CAESAR. I'll tell what I'll do. I'll break it in two and I'll eat half.

> *(He breaks it in half and eats one and bugs his eyes out and makes a big comic chewing sound of delight. Hesitantly, she eats the other half. At first she makes a face that it tastes disgusting but then gradually she shows that she likes it and licks her lips.)*

CAESAR. What do you think?

CLEOPATRA. I like it. *(Giggles.)* Gee, you're a funny old man.

CAESAR. The way you're perched on my knee, you remind me of a silky Persian cat. From where do you get your flame colored tresses?

CLEOPATRA. It's an ancient Egyptian secret.

CAESAR. Reveal it to me.

CLEOPATRA. I daren't. It is a sacred secret.

CAESAR. Do tell. I'll give you a shiny gold piece.

CLEOPATRA. How about a kiss?

CAESAR. I'm too old for that.

CLEOPATRA. No, you're not. You're not at all.

> *(They kiss.)*

CAESAR. Now tell me the secret of your ruby red hair.

CLEOPATRA. A cup of henna to a gallon of water.

CAESAR. I beg your pardon.

CLEOPATRA. You've never heard of Egyptian henna?

CAESAR. No, I haven't.

CLEOPATRA. You've got a lot to learn.

CAESAR. And there is much I could teach you. Cleopatra, do you appreciate history?

CLEOPATRA. I like stories. Someday you shall be a story. And so shall I.

CAESAR. You are so young. My story has mostly been told.

CLEOPATRA. It's not over. Make me a part of your story.

CAESAR. You must have heard that I have a wife, the noble Calpurnia.

CLEOPATRA. And?

CAESAR. She is my wife.

CLEOPATRA. One hears that she is a river that has run dry. She has made you childless.

CAESAR. I see no reason to discuss this further.

CLEOPATRA. My breasts are filled with love and life. My hips are rounded and well apart. Such women have sons and sons build empires.

CAESAR. So at last you have told me what you want of me.

CLEOPATRA. Out of us. We will succeed with your dreams. Your ambitions. One world. Our world.

CAESAR. *(Assessing her.)* I think perhaps I can make a queen of you at that.

CLEOPATRA. But I am a queen.

CAESAR. A true queen. A queen of substance and honor.

CLEOPATRA. Yes, that is my destiny. My Lord, make of me as you desire me.

(*The* SOOTHSAYER *enters.*)

SOOTHSAYER. Prophecies! Prophecies! Mine is the gift of prophecy.

CAESAR. Ah, the Soothsayer. What brilliant news of the future are you here to give me?

SOOTHSAYER. Caesar, as supreme as you are, you will know far greater triumph.

CLEOPATRA. You see what I told you?

CAESAR. For such a fine prophecy, I shall reward you with ten dinera.

SOOTHSAYER. *(Quick to anger.)* My gift of prophecy cannot be bought and sold. You degrade me! I spit on your coins!

CLEOPATRA. He was just being polite. You gave your forecast. Now kindly depart.

SOOTHSAYER. There is more. And not for Caesar. For you, royal Egypt.

CLEOPATRA. A message for me? Yeah?

SOOTHSAYER. *(Searching his soul for a vision.)* I see... I see...a vision. It's cloudy. You are making an entrance.

CLEOPATRA. What am I wearing?

SOOTHSAYER. A gown of solid gold.

CLEOPATRA. Sounds heavy but proceed.

SOOTHSAYER. I see a triumphant entrance to Rome. Thousands line the streets to greet you as a Goddess. But alas, you shall also know bitter defeat.

CLEOPATRA. You Soothsayers are all the same. You had to give me the last part so I'll come back for more.

SOOTHSAYER. *(Suddenly has a new vision.)* A girl. I see a young girl.

CLEOPATRA. Well, that's me.

SOOTHSAYER. A younger girl.

CLEOPATRA. Oh.

SOOTHSAYER. She has a mole.

CLEOPATRA. I have a mole.

SOOTHSAYER. This girl has ten moles.

CLEOPATRA. That's not me.

SOOTHSAYER. Treasure her. She will be of great importance to you.

> **(CHARMION,** *a beautiful young girl, enters carrying a shallow bowl of figs.)*

CHARMION. Pardon me. I have been sent to provide you, Great Caesar, with a small repast.

CAESAR. How thoughtful. I am feeling rather peckish. What have you?

CHARMION. Figs, my Lord. Plump and juicy. Freshly picked from the Ficus tree.

SOOTHSAYER. FIGS! FIGS! I have a vision of figs!

CLEOPATRA. Yeah, there they are. In that bowl.

SOOTHSAYER. Different figs. Years from now. A ghastly vision. No! No! Do not make me see!!

CAESAR. Well, at the moment, I shall take one of *these* figs. I am quite famished.

(He's about to dip his hand into the bowl of figs.)

CHARMION. August One, I have no doubt that you are as gracious as you are brave, but should you not ask the young lady to dip her hand first into the bowl of figs?

CAESAR. How piggish of me. My dear?

CLEOPATRA. Don't mind if I do.

*(**CLEOPATRA** is about to dip her hand into the bowl of figs. Suddenly, **CHARMION** stops her.)*

CHARMION. No! Don't! You mustn't!!

CAESAR. What goes with you, child? Are you mad?

CHARMION. There is hidden among the figs a venomous snake. One bite delivers instant death. Your Highness, I am to blame. Chop off my head. Disembowel me. I am yours to butcher.

CLEOPATRA. Yet, you saved my life. You stopped me from touching those figs. But why?

CHARMION. I was sent here by your brother, King Ptolemy. You were followed. He has spies everywhere. They found me on the streets. A prostitute. I was desperate, hungry and without friends or family. I took their evil money and pledged to provide them with your death. Kill me! Kill me! Plunge a dagger into my heart. I do not deserve to breathe the same air as you, most ravishing and exquisite of all human beings.

CLEOPATRA. What's your name, honey?

CHARMION. Charmion.

CLEOPATRA. Look, Char, it's not easy in this world for any female, royal or otherwise.

CHARMION. But to bring death to one so fair. You with your delicate features, your slim figure and your lustrous ruby red hair.

CLEOPATRA. Well, don't beat yourself up.

CAESAR. My dear, a Queen must fight against sentiment. This girl, contrite though she may be, should be brought to the executioner and swiftly.

CLEOPATRA. Wait a minute. What was that prophecy? *(Snaps her fingers.)* I was gonna meet a girl with ten moles.

CHARMION. I don't have ten moles.

CLEOPATRA. But you got ten count 'em ten freckles. Soothsayer, that's good enough for me. Caesar, I want this girl saved and couldn't you put her on the payroll? It would please me so.

CHARMION. What?

SOOTHSAYER. What?

CAESAR. I am frankly dubious of the child's change of heart, but we shall see that she is well taken care of.

CLEOPATRA. Thank you, Julius.

CAESAR. If you will excuse me, I must convene with my Generals. Cleopatra, we shall speak anon.

      *(**CAESAR** exits.)*

SOOTHSAYER. *(With great sentiment.)* That was a *very* beautiful thing to do.

CLEOPATRA. Okay, you. Out with it. Was it my brother who put you up to this or his cronies?

CHARMION. Your brother, King Ptolemy. He personally gave the order.

CLEOPATRA. I thought so. Ptolemy has gone too far. He's tried to murder me twice in one week. That karma lovin' son of a bitch isn't gettin' a third chance.

SOOTHSAYER. You must rid your heart of vengeance.

CLEOPATRA. You're annoying me but you're a good one to have around. I'm putting you also on the payroll.

SOOTHSAYER. My sacred gifts are not to be bartered. I shall not be insulted. I spit upon your gold coins!

CLEOPATRA. Shut up, Eight ball, and listen. Charmion, you're going to find me the whiskers of a black cougar. We'll chop 'em up and you'll put them in my brother's food. The sharp whiskers will perforate Ptolemy's intestines, providing a painful but untraceable death.

CHARMION. Done.

CLEOPATRA. Here's where you come in, Ouija. You'll use your gift of prophecy to tell us when the coast is clear. You can give us a five minute warning.

SOOTHSAYER. I cahn't! I cahn't! I cahn't!

(*The* **SOOTHSAYER** *runs off in hysteria.*)

CLEOPATRA. He'll be back.

CHARMION. Your Majesty, I think I've got a connection to get you them whiskers.

CLEOPATRA. Good girl. We need to work swiftly. Honey, this is what we're gonna do.

(*She puts her arm around* **CHARMION** *'s waist and the two dames exit.*)

End of Scene

Scene Two

*(CAESAR's villa in Rome. CAESAR enters with
ANTONY and OCTAVIAN. ANTONY announces
"Caesar's villa in Rome." Lights shift.)*

CAESAR. You plague me with your good intentions. I will
hear no more! No more!

ANTONY. Then listen to the voice of the people!

OCTAVIAN. They are greatly disturbed by your mad
infatuation with the Egyptian Queen.

CAESAR. The people adore Cleopatra. Her entrance into
Rome atop that monumental gold sphinx was the
greatest spectacle since Romulus and Remus. Women
and eunuchs, young and old, are copying her eye
makeup.

OCTAVIAN. That's all well and good, but her state visit was
to be for a fortnight.

ANTONY. It's now six months to the day.

OCTAVIAN. No one expected her to set up housekeeping
and arrange for laundry service.

ANTONY. Great Caesar, I implore you. Give her one more
good fuck and send her packing.

CAESAR. The Queen of Egypt is a visiting dignitary and
must be treated with the utmost respect.

OCTAVIAN. No woman is respected who is rumored to have
murdered her own brother.

CAESAR. Her brother was a deranged despot and besides he
died of a rupture to the intestine. A beautiful woman is
always the subject of gossip.

OCTAVIAN. Is it mere gossip that the Egyptian Queen
is encouraging you to turn the Republic into a
dictatorship?

CAESAR. I thought you knew me better than that.
Cleopatra's infatuation with me is a very useful tool.

ANTONY. I'll say it again, Caesar. Don't make her your
consort. Just ball her.

CAESAR. Watch yourself, Antony. Even a beloved protégé can overstep his position.

OCTAVIAN. Antony speaks out of the deepest respect. As we all do. There is also widespread affection for your noble wife Calpurnia. The citizens of Rome do not think kindly of a leader who brings disgrace to this woman of great dignity.

CAESAR. Calpurnia is contentedly ensconced in her villa in Pompeii. She has the good sense to keep her own council. Now, if you men will excuse me, I must occupy myself with something other than idle gossip.

 *(**CAESAR** exits.)*

OCTAVIAN. If the people turn on Caesar, they could very well turn on his Senate as well.

 *(**CLEOPATRA** enters unseen by **ANTONY** and **OCTAVIAN**. She listens to them plotting against her.)*

ANTONY. As long as Calpurnia is in Pompeii, Caesar feels free to corn hole the Egyptian whore.

OCTAVIAN. I have persuaded my Great Aunt Calpurnia to return immediately to Rome. Perhaps a virtuous wife is the best foil against the overblown charms of the sluttish serpent of the Nile.

 *(**CLEOPATRA** reveals her presence.)*

CLEOPATRA. You boys certainly know how to make a girl feel welcomed.

OCTAVIAN. Madame, you cut me to the quick. You will permit me to withdraw.

 *(He bows and exits. **ANTONY** is about to follow him.)*

ANTONY. I too should be on my way.

CLEOPATRA. Not so fast, Muscles. You've had it in for me ever since we met in Tarsus. What did I ever do to you?

ANTONY. It is what you are doing to great Caesar and to Rome that concerns me. You don't love Caesar.

CLEOPATRA. You couldn't be more wrong. I do love Caesar. I love him very much. More than I ever thought possible.

ANTONY. He's old enough to be your grandfather.

CLEOPATRA. I must admit to being stimulated by his... gravitas. Caesar has taught me statesmanship. He has taught me diplomacy. He has taught me how to love.

ANTONY. He hasn't taught you to respect a man's marriage.

CLEOPATRA. I've been taught by experts never to trust any man's fidelity.

ANTONY. For a Daughter of the Sun and Moon, that sounds almost human. Someday you may grow a woman's heart and it will bring about your doom.

CLEOPATRA. That sounds almost sympathetic.

ANTONY. It wasn't meant to be.

CLEOPATRA. Why should you be different from anyone else? I've never felt as lonely as I have here in Rome this spring.

ANTONY. The answer to your social dilemma might be simply...to leave. *(He bows.)* Madame.

> *(ANTONY starts to leave just as the imperious, imposing CALPURNIA enters.)*

ANTONY. Your most honorable Mistress Calpurnia. I was just taking my leave.

CALPURNIA. Tribune, I trust we shall dine later this evening.

ANTONY. That would give me great pleasure.

> *(ANTONY bows and exits.)*

CALPURNIA. By your lush overripe beauty, I presume you to be Cleopatra, Queen of the Nile.

CLEOPATRA. And by your monumental grandeur, I would presume you to be Caesar's noble wife Calpurnia.

CALPURNIA. I thank you for qualifying my name with that of my husband.

CLEOPATRA. If I had known that you were returning from Pompeii, I would have had my servants plan a feast in your honor.

CALPURNIA. That would be most inappropriate since this is my home.

CLEOPATRA. And lovely it is. I so admire your taste in home furnishings. Everything really works.

CALPURNIA. Perhaps you also admire my taste in husbands.

CLEOPATRA. Hard for me to say. I wouldn't know how he is as a husband.

CALPURNIA. But there is much you do know of Caesar. Rather intimately, I would surmise.

CLEOPATRA. I cannot control the gossiping tongues of the Roman senate.

CALPURNIA. Do not underestimate yourself, my dear. I'm sure you're quite the expert on men's tongues.

CLEOPATRA. Oh, so you wanna roll around in the sawdust, do ya? Well, Egyptian royalty doesn't perform in a circus.

CALPURNIA. You may wear the silken robes of a queen, but they fool no one.

CLEOPATRA. They're beautiful robes but when great Caesar doesn't like what I wear, I take it off.

CALPURNIA. You don't have a streak of decency in you.

CLEOPATRA. I don't show my good points to strangers.

CALPURNIA. This sordid liaison with Caesar must come to an end immediately. You will return to Egypt.

CLEOPATRA. Says who? I forge my own destiny. And it appears in the prophecies of my Soothsayer that Caesar's destiny and mine are one.

CALPURNIA. Your Soothsayer? This is barbaric absurdity.

CLEOPATRA. So far the predictions have been one hundred percent accurate and that's good enough odds for me.

CALPURNIA. You will bring about Caesar's downfall.

CLEOPATRA. I beg to differ. With my help, he shall be crowned Emperor.

CALPURNIA. That goes against his every belief.

CLEOPATRA. A true leader grows and acquires new beliefs. I shall make of him a divinity.

CALPURNIA. You've succeeded in making him a figure of ridicule. Don't fool yourself into thinking he loves you. He just imagines he does.

CLEOPATRA. I will admit the great man has a vivid imagination.

CALPURNIA. Like most men, he's merely amusing himself with a harlot.

CLEOPATRA. My ancestors on my mother's side were all big cats. Don't get me sore.

CALPURNIA. I have discretion and propriety on my side.

CLEOPATRA. A man needs a lot more than discretion and propriety from a wife.

CALPURNIA. I won't listen to such vulgarity.

CLEOPATRA. You'll listen, Iceberg, and you'll listen good. With you turning his bed into the frozen tundra, you made him old before his time. I found out there's plenty of starch left in him. With me, he can perform all night, all morning and then surprise me with it in the afternoon.

CALPURNIA. I must leave this den of perversion at once!

CLEOPATRA. I'm not finished with you.

CALPURNIA. You have taken enough from me and I refuse to give you anything more, not even one more minute.

(CALPURNIA exits. CLEOPATRA calls out to CHARMION.)

CLEOPATRA. Charmion!

(CHARMION enters.)

CHARMION. Mistress?

CLEOPATRA. Fetch me a fig.

End of Scene

Scene Three

(The actor playing **ACHMED** *announces "A street in Rome." The lights shift and a bearded and turbaned Arab,* **ACHMED**, *is followed by a beautiful young girl named* **IRAS**. *She's toting on her back an enormous satchel almost as big as she is.)*

ACHMED. Girl, pick up your feet. We still have a ways to go.

IRAS. Please, Achmed, I need rest. We have been walking for three days.

ACHMED. You will rest when we reach the house of your new master.

IRAS. How much further?

ACHMED. His villa is on the seventh hill of Rome.

IRAS. We've already walked up and down six. My feet are one big blister.

ACHMED. Stop that moaning or I'll... *(He raises his hand as if to strike her.)*

IRAS. No, no, please don't strike me. If I'm bruised and battered my intended may not take me.

ACHMED. The Merchant Abatelli has promised me a hundred dinera to provide him with a young bride. He'll pay for whatever I deliver.

IRAS. He won't pay for a dead girl. And I will surely perish unless I have some water.

ACHMED. Stay here. I'll look around and see if I can find a well. And don't you get any fancies of escaping.

IRAS. I won't. I have nowhere to run.

> *(**ACHMED** exits. **IRAS** bursts into tears. **CHARMION** enters balancing a jug on her shoulder. She sees **IRAS** sitting on her satchel sobbing.)*

CHARMION. Is there something wrong?

IRAS. No. Yes. No. I'll be all right.

CHARMION. I can't imagine any sight more pitiful than you there, alone, sittin' on your satchel. Would you like something to drink on this sultry morning?

IRAS. Bless you, kind soul. I desperately need something to wet my parched lips.

CHARMION. Here. Partake of this refreshing water. And I can give you some lip balm as well.

IRAS. I cannot thank you enough.

(**CHARMION** *gives* **IRAS** *the jug and* **IRAS** *drinks from it.*)

CHARMION. Have you been traveling a long distance?

IRAS. Yes, all the way from Cypress. I have been sold to a Roman merchant. I am to be his bride. I have never met him. I am told he is a cruel and brutal man. So is the flesh monger who arranged the purchase. He will be back soon. You had better go before he returns. He will flog us both.

CHARMION. Let him try. I am the handmaiden of the Queen of Egypt.

IRAS. Cleopatra? The poisonous serpent of the Nile?

CHARMION. She is a much maligned lady and a more decent employer you never will find.

IRAS. I have heard tales that she is an evil sorceress and has drunk the semen of a thousand seamen.

CHARMION. Don't believe a word of that malarkey. Look, we're understaffed here in Rome. She could use a new girl. Have you any skills?

IRAS. I'm a manicurist by trade.

CHARMION. That she could use. Do you do hair?

IRAS. Not really. But I'm a fast learner. I'm something of a perfectionist.

CHARMION. I think we can make this work. You'll be the second assistant.

IRAS. Then we should leave immediately. The brute might return at any moment.

CHARMION. Don't you need anything in that bag?

IRAS. Eh. It's all crap. I can never thank you enough for coming to my aid. Generous friend, I don't even know your name.

CHARMION. Charmion. And yours?

IRAS. Iras. I can't remember when I last spoke my name. I have been beaten into silent submission.

CHARMION. You have nothing to fear in the household of Queen Cleopatra as long as you always speak the truth to her.

IRAS. I'm so shy. I doubt I'll ever utter a word in her presence.

CHARMION. We had best not tarry. Let's make a run for it.

(*The two girls run offstage.*)

End of Scene

Scene Four

(The actor playing **CHARMION** *announces* "**CLEOPATRA**'s *boudoir in Rome." The lights shift.* **CLEOPATRA** *is lounging on her divan.* **APOLLODORUS** *is standing behind her cooling her off with a large fan.* **CHARMION** *is furiously brushing out a long "switch" of hair, belonging to the Queen.* **IRAS** *is filing the Queen's nails and regaling her with bawdy gossip. Both* **CLEOPATRA** *and* **APOLLODORUS** *are laughing and greatly enjoying her company.* **CHARMION** *is not amused.)*

IRAS. The way I heard it the prostitute's pussy was stretched to the limit. It's that Mark Antony. His cock is so huge. They say it's like a python. And he couldn't get it out. He was literally stuck inside the whore. He tried pushing her away, "Get offa me. Get offa me!"

CLEOPATRA. *(Laughing.)* Stop! Stop! I can't take anymore.

IRAS. That's what the whore said. So the brothel keeper got the ugliest scraggliest old woman in the house, a toothless hag who scrubs the floors, to sit on his face so he he'd lose his hard on. And it didn't work. Mark Antony loves pussy any way he can get it. Queen, it took them almost two days to get his big gorgonzola out of that whore's twat.

CLEOPATRA. This one makes me laugh. I like her. Before I forget, Charmion, didja send that papyrus scroll over to the pyramid architect? Those things take ninety years to build. I wanna get him started.

CHARMION. Your Majesty, please forgive me. I intended to but I spent much of the day mending your...

IRAS. Charmion was so busy, I delivered the scroll. I should have told you, Charmion.

CHARMION. Yes, you should have.

CLEOPATRA. What does it matter? Thank you, Iras. Charmion, be careful brushing that thing. It's a hundred percent human hair. I'm under a lot of pressure today. Caesar's making an important speech at the Forum. He's going to announce that he's decided to give himself a new title; God. My idea.

APOLLODORUS. I didn't think he was gonna announce it so soon.

CLEOPATRA. Word got out. Nowadays you can't keep anything a secret.

APOLLODORUS. You think there'll be trouble?

CLEOPATRA. You never know with these Romans. They'll stick a knife in you over a plate of ziti.

CHARMION. When Caesar returns from the Forum, I'm sure your highness will want to look her best.

CLEOPATRA. That's the general idea.

CHARMION. I took the precaution of cleaning your ruby necklace.

IRAS. The Queen is not going to want to wear her rubies tonight.

CLEOPATRA. No?

IRAS. Tonight is for emeralds to bring out the green in Her Majesty's eyes.

CLEOPATRA. He is crazy about my eyes.

CHARMION. Iras, you have not been granted permission to touch the Queen's jewels.

IRAS. That is true. Forgive me but I saw how busy you were mending the ceremonial robe.

CHARMION. I wasn't that busy. I can do several things at once.

IRAS. We've all been worried that you've been working too hard.

CHARMION. You've been gossiping about me as well? Who's "we?"

IRAS. You nearly bit off Doris's head when she tried to help you.

CHARMION. Hey, hey, hey. And where do you get off calling him "Doris?"

APOLLODORUS. I told her it was all right if said with love.

CHARMION. Oh, so now you two love each other? She's been here less than a week.

IRAS. I appreciated his kindness.

CHARMION. That's a dig at me, I suppose.

IRAS. Well, maybe it is.

CLEOPATRA. That's enough, girls.

CHARMION. I've never seen such ingratitude. I picked you up off the street. I got you cleaned up, picked the bugs out of your coozie, gave you makeup tips so you'd look human, introduced you to the Queen, got you on the payroll. And the minute you arrived, you started plotting to take my place.

IRAS. You're out of your mind. You never picked anything out of my coozie.

CHARMION. What did you think I was doing with that tweezers? Mining for silver?

IRAS. Getting your kicks. You've been licking your lips over my titties ever since you saw me on the Appian Way.

CLEOPATRA. All right, you two.

CHARMION. I felt sorry for you, sister, but not anymore. And give me back those earrings you "borrowed" off of me.

> (*She tries to rip them off her ears.* IRAS *pushes her away.*)

IRAS. These are my earrings, Leprosy fingers. Maybe if you weren't blind as a fucking bat, you'd see the difference.

CHARMION. I'll show you they're mine! And I'll rip your ugly elephant ears off to get 'em!

> (*She tries again to grab* IRAS' *ear. The two girls begin to cat fight.* CLEOPATRA *claps her hands.* APOLLODORUS *puts down his fan and tries to separate the two girls.*)

CLEOPATRA. Girls! Girls! I will have none of this! Not in my divine presence.

(**APOLLODORUS** *separates them. The two girls bow deeply in supplication.*)

CHARMION. Do forgive us, Your Majesty.

IRAS. We bow our heads in the deepest of shame.

CLEOPATRA. We're guests of the Romans. We must always show them our best. I suppose with Caesar speaking at the Forum, all of our nerves are ragged.

(*The* **SOOTHSAYER** *enters.*)

SOOTHSAYER. Your Majesty, if I may take a moment of your time.

CLEOPATRA. This is all I need. Now what?

SOOTHSAYER. (*Greatly agitated.*) My eyes are burning with a prophecy. It consumes me with a fever.

CLEOPATRA. All right. Calm down. Everyone's in a lather today.

SOOTHSAYER. May we speak in private?

CLEOPATRA. If we must. Girls, you may withdraw. Go outside and cool yourselves off. Doris, watch 'em.

(**APOLLODORUS, CHARMION** *and* **IRAS** *bow deeply and exit.*)

CLEOPATRA. What's on your mind?

SOOTHSAYER. My gift of prophecy is a curse. I've been called a liar, a sham, a fake. And when I'm proven correct, my prophecies are dismissed as mere coincidence. Coincidence. That word! That evil word!

CLEOPATRA. All right. Your life is miserable. I'm running late. Make it fast.

SOOTHSAYER. Let me touch your belly.

CLEOPATRA. No!

SOOTHSAYER. There is life within you. A child to be born of you and Caesar.

CLEOPATRA. Life? I am carrying great Caesar's child?

SOOTHSAYER. You will be bearing him a son.

CLEOPATRA. A son. An heir. You're sure you got this right?

SOOTHSAYER. You doubting me? Why do I even bother?

CLEOPATRA. I'm sorry. I'm sorry. So this is what you wanted to tell me?

SOOTHSAYER. No. This thing about the baby just came to me in a flash. I have other news to impart.

CLEOPATRA. More good news, I hope?

SOOTHSAYER. No, terrible news. The worst news possible. Beware of the Ides of March.

CLEOPATRA. Why? What happens then?

SOOTHSAYER. I see a vision. Caesar at the Forum. He has come to address the Senate. *(Takes a dramatic pause.)* Caesar is to be assassinated! He must be warned!

CLEOPATRA. When are the Ides of March?

SOOTHSAYER. March 15th.

CLEOPATRA. March 15th? Today is March 15th, you nitwit! And Caesar's at the Forum right now!! I see it all before me. Like the colors in a flame. My love. My great love.

> *(Behind her, a pair of doors opens and bathed in red light we see* **CAESAR** *being stabbed by three robed figures. He cries out "Et tu Brute?" The doors close.* **CHARMION**, **IRAS** *and* **APOLLODORUS** *rush on stage.* **IRAS** *is holding the switch of hair.)*

CHARMION. Royal Egypt! A terrible tragedy has occurred.

APOLLODORUS. Caesar has been murdered!

IRAS. He was stabbed twenty-three times by his own senators.

CLEOPATRA. Where is hc? Where is Caesar?

CHARMION. He lies at the foot of Pompey's statue. No one will touch the body.

CLEOPATRA. I will. Take me to him.

APOLLODORUS. Majesty, the mob is on its way. They cry for Egypt's blood. We must escape. They will kill you.

CLEOPATRA. I don't care.

CHARMION. Think of Egypt.

CLEOPATRA. Always Egypt. Caesar is dead. My lover is dead.

APOLLODORUS. Caesar never loved you.

CLEOPATRA. You lie! You lie! Give me that switch! *(IRAS gives her a braid of hair.* **CLEOPATRA** *is about to whip him with it.)*

APOLLODORUS. Majesty!!

(She drops the switch, and collapses into his arms.)

It wasn't in his arms he wanted to hold Egypt. It was in his treasury.

SOOTHSAYER. He speaks the truth. Majesty, at last you must open your eyes.

IRAS. Royal Egypt, you were sightless as all women are when they wish to be loved.

CLEOPATRA. It will never happen again. We must flee to Egypt at once.

CHARMION. Iras, help me pack up the wiglets.

CLEOPATRA. Leave 'em. We can pick up new hair in Memphis.

End of Scene

Scene Five

(OCTAVIAN, ANTONY and the ROMAN SENATOR LEPIDUS enter. OCTAVIAN steps into the light and announces "Rome, a chamber off of the Senate.")

OCTAVIAN. Antony! Antony! Always Antony. I have had quite enough of Antony!

ANTONY. Octavian, sit down.

OCTAVIAN. That's all I do is sit. I'm sitting so much I'm getting Secretary's spread.

ANTONY. You see, Lepidus, he makes a fuss even about sitting.

OCTAVIAN. I also object to your patronizing tone, sir. I am no longer your simpering adolescent admirer. I am your equal. I am more than your equal. I am Caesar's legitimate heir.

(ANTONY makes a disrespectful raspberry sound.)

LEPIDUS. Antony, Octavian! The Senate has decreed that the three of us should form a triumvirate and govern Rome as one. It has been decided in the best interests of the state that Antony be in command of waging war on Egypt.

OCTAVIAN. But why Antony? I have proved myself most adept with the sword and the shield.

ANTONY. I'll govern with you but if there is any fighting to be done I'll do it alone.

OCTAVIAN. You see? I am always shut out. You want to do everything alone. You have no ideals beyond promoting yourself. You used my uncle's dead body to win control. Holding up his blood stained toga like any ham play actor to make the crowd cheer you. You with your "Friends, Romans, Countrymen!"

(ANTONY rises as if to strike him. OCTAVIAN cowers. LEPIDUS restrains ANTONY.)

LEPIDUS. Steady.

ANTONY. I accept the Senate's orders.

LEPIDUS. Good. And you, Octavian?

OCTAVIAN. Oh, what does it matter what I think? And how do you propose, oh brave one, to punish Egypt?

ANTONY. I shall write a letter to the Egyptian Queen demanding that she meet me in the public square in Tarsus.

OCTAVIAN. A letter? Now that does tickle me. The great warrior Mark Antony fights with friendly notes? On pink stationary, I presume?

ANTONY. Octavian is right for once. It will only give the impression of a "friendly" note.

LEPIDUS. I see. She will be led to believe the meeting a friendly discussion on Roman and Egyptian affairs. Cleopatra may be a Queen but like all women she thinks only with her heart.

ANTONY. Yes. She will be lulled by the conciliatory tone of my missive.

OCTAVIAN. Pray, go on. I'm fascinated.

ANTONY. The Queen will be instructed to meet me in the public square in Tarsus at noon. What she will not know is that she will be taken from Tarsus to Rome... in chains.

End of Scene

Scene Six

(CLEOPATRA's barge. IRAS and CHARMION enter. The actor playing IRAS announces "CLEOPATRA's barge at sea." The two girls are spraying perfume with large atomizers around the large divan. They are barely speaking to each other.)

CHARMION. Arrange those pillows, if it's not too much trouble for you.

IRAS. *(Rolling her eyes.)* Look, I've gotta get something off my chest. I came here after being brutalized by heartless, cruel men. You've experienced the same, not as a bartered bride but, you know, being a street whore. I hoped and prayed that I'd find here a safe harbor. No such luck. You've made my life absolutely miserable. I still don't know what I did wrong.

CHARMION. You can't figure that out, huh? I've taken you for a bitch but never a fool. However, perhaps I was the greater fool for allowing you to plot and scheme against me.

IRAS. I can't help it if I'm a big personality. Her Majesty likes having me around. Maybe she found you, dare I say, wanting.

CHARMION. She found me reliable, trustworthy and steadfast.

IRAS. That sounds like a lot of laughs.

CHARMION. Wanna laugh? How about some perfume in your puss? *(She sprays her in the face.)*

IRAS. Don't do that.

CHARMION. Take some more!

(CHARMION sprays her again.)

IRAS. I warned you.

(CHARMION sprays her again.)

CHARMION. Take some more!

(**IRAS** *picks up the other atomizer and sprays* **CHARMION** *in the face. They begin cat fighting again. Suddenly, they pause and begin passionately kissing. They break apart.*)

CHARMION. What have we done?

IRAS. I believe we have committed a sin. Are we the same as those perverse women in Sodom and Gomorrah?

CHARMION. The ones who play golf? That couldn't be us. They have thick hairy ankles and we darken our eyes with kohl and stain our lips with berry juice.

IRAS. And yet all this time, I have dreamed of nothing else but burying my face in your fertile crescent.

CHARMION. Shhhh. You mustn't say that.

IRAS. It's true! It's true! I am guilty of that desire. There I said it. I feel so dirty!!!

CHARMION. I must confess I too have dreamed of exploring the abundance of your luxuriant mossy bank.

IRAS. Have you ever kissed a girl before?

CHARMION. No. Never. Have you?

IRAS. Not me. No. That's a lie. Years ago I canoodled with a High Priestess with big knockers. It was a festival day and we'd been drinkin'. I wouldn't mind trying it again. Is that perfectly dreadful of me?

CHARMION. Nothing about you could be dreadful. Oh, Iras, all this time wasted in bitter conflict, merely because we were masquerading our true feelings. How foolish we were.

IRAS. So foolish. What happens now?

CHARMION. Shall we throw caution to the four winds and derive comfort within the bosom of our own sex?

IRAS. Oh yes, my love. But the Queen must never know. She will be furious.

CHARMION. Her? That dame was married to her own brother. She's not one to pass judgement.

IRAS. I hadn't thought of that.

CHARMION. Cleopatra had this barge built as a vehicle of seduction. Let us use this voyage for our own journey into a sea of desire.

IRAS. When Her Majesty goes to bed, I shall find my way to your chamber. Till then, my darling Charmion.

> *(They kiss and **IRAS** runs off. **CHARMION** is breathless and begins frantically spraying more perfume around the room. **CLEOPATRA** enters in a gown and headdress both magnificent and seductive.)*

CLEOPATRA. Charmion, I think you overdid it with the perfume. I smell something else in here. This dense pungent aroma reminds me of a back room on the island of Lesbos.

CHARMION. I um can't imagine why. *(Quickly changing the subject.)* I am told by the captain that we will soon be approaching Tarsus.

CLEOPATRA. Are we?

CHARMION. And no plans yet for disembarking? Forgive me for being so bold, but I'm frightened. If this meeting with the Tribune Mark Antony fails, it means slavery for Egypt...and death for you. Where are you to meet Mark Antony?

CLEOPATRA. I was told to meet him in the public square at noon.

CHARMION. But, Mistress, that was six hours ago.

CLEOPATRA. Well, how about that? We silly women do spend endless hours fussing with our maquillage. Where does the time fly?

> *(A trumpet is heard signaling **ANTONY**'s arrival on the barge.)*

That must be Antony. The great warrior has come to me. How am I doing?

CHARMION. I'd say you were doing just grand.

CLEOPATRA. I'd say I'd have to agree with you. Send the sucker – I mean the gentleman in.

(**CHARMION** *exits.* **CLEOPATRA** *arranges the train of her gown. Haunting music and a vision appears. It is* **CAESAR***'s ghost.*)

CAESAR. Cleopatra.

CLEOPATRA. A strange apparition appears before me. Are you Osiris, the god of the underworld and the afterlife?

CAESAR. Never a God. I was for a moment named a deity and that alas was my downfall. Pride and arrogance were my handmaidens. Do you not recognize me? Have I so changed?

CLEOPATRA. It's kind of fuzzy. Like peering through a veil of Egyptian cotton with a two hundred thread count.

CAESAR. It is I, Egypt. Gaze upon the remains of he who was once Julius Caesar.

CLEOPATRA. Caesar? But why should you haunt me? I was not among the traitors who slew you.

CAESAR. Of that I am most clear. I see now in death that Cleopatra was the only one who truly loved me.

CLEOPATRA. About time. After all, I am the mother of your child.

CAESAR. I thank you for bringing forth from your fruitful loins my one and only son.

CLEOPATRA. It wasn't easy. I call him Caesarian. And he is fine little boy with the qualities of a future King.

CAESAR. It almost warms my cold shade to hear that. Cleopatra, my ghostly travails will be less arduous to endure if I am able to provide you with the wisdom of my years on earth.

CLEOPATRA. Give it to me straight.

CAESAR. Antony has climbed aboard this barge to escort you to your doom.

CLEOPATRA. Yes, I know. Through my cunning, he boards this ship alone and vulnerable. Score one for me.

CAESAR. But now I must warn you not to succumb to his virile charms. Women find him irresistible.

CLEOPATRA. Not this one. However, I shall fool the great Antony into believing that I'm falling for him. I will appeal to his legendary vanity. His Achilles heel, so to speak. Remember that jerk?

CAESAR. Be vigilant, Egypt, and mouth your plangent words of love but in your heart feel nothing. You have the mind of a king. Rely on your intellect, Cleopatra. That will be your salvation.

CLEOPATRA. I seek to make you proud, O Spirit.

CAESAR. I fear I am being called away by the vapor of the great Pompey. I must go. I must go.

CLEOPATRA. When shall I see you next?

CAESAR. When you are once more at a dangerous crossroads. It is my hope that you will never require my council and never again see my ghostly visage.

CLEOPATRA. Caesar!

(**CAESAR** *exits.* **APOLLODORUS** *enters.*)

APOLLODORUS. Royal Egypt.

CLEOPATRA. Yes, Appollodurus?

APOLLODORUS. The Tribune Mark Antony, Your Majesty.

(**MARK ANTONY** *enters as if dressed for battle, with a breast plate and carrying his helmet.*)

CLEOPATRA. Well, look who the sphinx dragged in.

ANTONY. We'll go now. Get ready.

CLEOPATRA. Were you speaking to me?

ANTONY. Who do you think?

CLEOPATRA. It's been a while so you might start with "How are you?"

ANTONY. I sent orders for you to come to the square. I am not used to being disobeyed.

CLEOPATRA. *(With an air of intimacy.)* Your letter said we had things to talk about. So let's talk.

ANTONY. That letter said we'd meet in the public square in Tarsus and that's where we are going. And we're taking the direct road. I've been warned of your dangerous curves.

CLEOPATRA. *(Purring.)* Mmmmm. We can't talk here?

ANTONY. No, we cannot talk here. It's too...distracting. The perfume too intoxicating.

CLEOPATRA. My girl did pour it on pretty thick. I must tell you why I wanted to meet you here instead of the square.

ANTONY. Well?

CLEOPATRA. You see the way I'm dressed?

ANTONY. What about it?

CLEOPATRA. I'm costumed to lure you, Antony. You have to admit it has a flash.

ANTONY. Aaaagh.

CLEOPATRA. You're so butch. You wouldn't know lamé from burlap. Well, this gown was all part of a plan to seduce you. It was my only chance to save myself. Do you know I had show after show with which to dazzle you? Girls, girls and more girls. Naked girls. Girls with wings. Girls in slings. Girls with toys. Girly boys. Girl on girl action. But Antony is not a man to be dazzled. No. What do you think about this for instance?

> *(She claps her hands and* **IRAS** *enters and performs an erotic dance.* **ANTONY** *fights to keep his face impassive.)*

I wish you could see your face. I'd have more chance with a stone wall.

> *(More dancing.* **CHARMION** *brings out a tray with a decanter of wine, a goblet and a small bud vase with a flower in it... After placing it down, she joins* **IRAS** *in performing a duo erotic and quite Sapphic dance.)*

Gee, I was bluffing about the girl on girl stuff. Didn't know that was on the bill.

> *(She claps her hands and the girls exit.)*

ANTONY. Well…shall we go now?

CLEOPATRA. Yes, we'll go. My wits have failed. But what could I do? Now what would you have done? Pretend you are me and I'm you. *(She takes the flower from the vase and sticks it behind his ear. He tries to remove it.)* No, no. You are Cleopatra and I'm Antony. *(She folds her arms and makes a glum face.)*

ANTONY. Do I look like that?

CLEOPATRA. Well, do I?

> *(She laughs and he joins her laughing.)*

ANTONY. I think you'd better stay as Cleopatra. *(He is about to drink from the goblet.)*

CLEOPATRA. Oh, no. Don't drink that. That was part of the plan too. I was going to get you so…irresponsible.

ANTONY. You don't think that one goblet would do it. Did you?

CLEOPATRA. Yes, wouldn't it?

ANTONY. *(Laughs.)* Well, that does amuse me.

> *(He drinks more.)*

CLEOPATRA. But it's such a large goblet. *(He keeps drinking.)*

ANTONY. Yes, isn't it? *(He drinks it all.)*

CLEOPATRA. *(Impressed.)* Well.

ANTONY. I hope you know that I know you want me to do this.

CLEOPATRA. Dear Antony, I hope you think I know you know.

ANTONY. I hope you think I know you know you know.

CLEOPATRA. Oh stop, please.

> *(They both laugh at their foolishness.)*

We're laughing. This is the last thing I expected. You bring something out in me that I thought had withered and died.

ANTONY. Nothing about you is dead and withered. You are life incarnate.

CLEOPATRA. I appreciate hearing you say that. I wouldn't mind hearing more.

> (CLEOPATRA *sings a fun sultry love song that wouldn't be out of place in a 1930s movie, such as "I Want You, I Need You" from the Mae West film* I'm No Angel.* *When she finishes the number, there's a new intimacy between* ANTONY *and* CLEOPATRA.)

CLEOPATRA. A song to the stars. They must think we're funny people. Scheming to destroy each other. As if we had forever to live.

ANTONY. I said things to Caesar I wish I hadn't.

CLEOPATRA. Oh?

ANTONY. There is beauty in the Egyptian Queen besides her face. Do you miss him?

CLEOPATRA. No. It's as if I only saw him moments ago. Besides, he didn't love me.

> (ANTONY *raises his glass to her.*)

ANTONY. I thank you for that. *(He drinks from his goblet and moves in closer to her. He kisses her hand.)* You're ravishing.

CLEOPATRA. Oh.

ANTONY. You're enchanting.

CLEOPATRA. Oh.

ANTONY. You're bewitching. You're tantalizing. You're delicious. You're fascinating. You're charming.

CLEOPATRA. *(Seductively.)* I've always heard you had an enormous...vocabulary. All right. I'm ready to go now.

ANTONY. Why? Oh, you don't find me charming?

---

*A license to produce *Charles Busch's Cleopatra* does not include a performance license for "I Want You, I Need You" The publisher and author suggest that the licensee contact ASCAP or BMI to ascertain the rights holder to acquire permission for performance of this song. If permission is unattainable, the licensee should create an original composition in a similar style. For further information, please see music use note on page 3

CLEOPATRA. Oh, yes I do. I could fall in love with you but I
    don't intend to. What for?

ANTONY. Do you mean that?

CLEOPATRA. Do I mean it?

> *(She reprises the end of her song.* ANTONY *nuzzles
> her neck.)*

Mmmmm. Lovely.

> (CLEOPATRA *nods to* APOLLODORUS. *The drapes
> are pulled, enveloping her and* ANTONY.*)*

End of Scene

Scene Seven

(Rome, **OCTAVIAN***'s villa.* **LEPIDUS** *enters with*
OCTAVIAN*'s beautiful and gentle twin sister,*
OCTAVIA. *The actor playing* **LEPIDUS** *announces*
"Rome, **OCTAVIAN***'s villa.")*

LEPIDUS. One of the advantages of meeting with Octavian
at his home is the chance of visiting with his lovely twin
sister. I hope I am not intruding upon your privacy,
young Octavia.

OCTAVIA. You are never an intrusion, dear Lepidus. I
look forward to any visit from you as a rose eagerly
anticipates the rising of the sun, as a wandering dog
seeks the affection of a wayfarer, as the parched earth
seeks the night's cool mist, as a log leaps to a flame and
as the raging fire bows gratefully before the rain.

LEPIDUS. My dear, is my presence truly of such importance
to you?

OCTAVIA. Oh, but it is. There are weeks when my brother
is away on business of state that I see no one but my
ancient nurse; the old Gorgon, with her walrus's
moustache, who sleeps at the foot of my bed. I do not
wish to appear ungrateful for my brother loves me so,
but I am as lonely and bereft as one incarcerated in
Mamertine Prison. If only to fly away from here on the
wings of Pegasus for even one day.

LEPIDUS. Oh, my dear. My dear.

OCTAVIA. Forgive me. It is dreadfully unfair of me to
burden you with my confidence.

LEPIDUS. It is not a burden, young Octavia. Be assured that
your brother only desires what is best for you.

OCTAVIA. Could he possibly be wrong? Perhaps what is
best for me is to be among people, to have friends, and
dare I say, even mild flirtations. I shock you with my
perversity.

LEPIDUS. No, it is only natural that one who is young and
lovely should desire the attentions of a suitor.

OCTAVIA. How and when shall I ever find such a suitor? There are times I think my brother is saving me as some sort of treasure to be bartered when the opportunity presents itself. Do forgive my impudence.

LEPIDUS. Octavia, a great marriage must not be entered into lightly.

OCTAVIA. I merely wish to be loved. I dream of a gentle soul who will patiently awaken me on my wedding night to the pleasures of Eros. Again, I shock you with my perversity.

LEPIDUS. Yes, I must admit, as a man whose soul is as dry as parchment, your passionate tone does rather unsettle one. Ah, I hear footsteps approaching. I imagine it to be your brother.

(The SOOTHSAYER *enters.)*

SOOTHSAYER. Do forgive me for entering unannounced. I was told this room was empty.

OCTAVIA. Oh, but it is. This chamber is inhabited by one who is rendered invisible.

LEPIDUS. You are the Soothsayer one hears much about.

SOOTHSAYER. I am most flattered.

OCTAVIA. Might you have a prophecy for me? I am in need of an encouraging prediction.

SOOTHSAYER. You should be pleased. I see a wedding bower in the very near future.

OCTAVIA. I am afraid, Soothsayer, in this instance, you are as accurate as a blind thief searching for an open window.

SOOTHSAYER. But I do see a marriage within months of today.

OCTAVIA. That is quite impossible and rather heartless of you to insist upon. Good day, Soothsayer, and Lepidus, I must thank you. Your visit has acted as a well needed restorative.

LEPIDUS. Good day, my lady.

*(***OCTAVIA*** exits.)*

SOOTHSAYER. Rarely have I laid eyes upon so mournful a beauty.

LEPIDUS. She is indeed a maiden shrouded in sadness. Pray, are you here to provide council to the August Octavian?

SOOTHSAYER. No, it is you, Lepidus, to whom I seek.

LEPIDUS. Well, here we are. Speak forth your prophecies. We shall see if they are mere fancies of a fevered brain.

SOOTHSAYER. May I speak frankly and without threat of prison?

LEPIDUS. I have no fear of a Soothsayer's tongue.

SOOTHSAYER. I have had a vision of good Lepidus being deposed.

LEPIDUS. Deposed? That is quite impossible. I am most secure in my alliance with Octavian.

SOOTHSAYER. Octavian is consumed with ambition to be the sole Emperor of Rome.

LEPIDUS. Your words reek of treason, but I promised you could speak freely.

SOOTHSAYER. I thank you, august one.

LEPIDUS. Octavian is a most complex young man but among his attributes is loyalty.

SOOTHSAYER. As a wandering prophet, I have been privileged to visit all of the royal kingdoms.

LEPIDUS. You have been to Egypt?

SOOTHSAYER. Indeed I have.

LEPIDUS. You have seen Antony and Cleopatra?

SOOTHSAYER. I have been in their presence. They are very much in love.

LEPIDUS. It is mad obsession. The serpent of the Nile holds him in her thrall. She is a creature of the most selfish desire.

SOOTHSAYER. She is a monarch who wishes only for peace among other monarchs.

LEPIDUS. She is a viper who seeks sensual dominance over all men. Perhaps you are a spy for the Egyptian Queen. A cosseted favorite of Cleopatra.

SOOTHSAYER. Definitely not a favorite. More than once she's whipped me with an auburn switch. Despite her vile temper, she seeks a world devoted to peace.

LEPIDUS. I wish I could believe that.

SOOTHSAYER. I have visions of this planet centuries from now. I see the Earth growing hot as coals from the greed of men. I see endless warring among nations. I see weaponry that in a single explosion can destroy the entire world. All of this can be avoided by simply being nice to Cleopatra.

LEPIDUS. You are a mad fool. I hear Octavian approaching. Even a mad fool deserves to live. You had best flee this residence. Off with you.

SOOTHSAYER. Do not dismiss my words.

LEPIDUS. Be gone! There is an egress just beyond that wall.

    (*The* **SOOTHSAYER** *runs off in one direction as* **OCTAVIAN** *enters from the opposite side.*)

OCTAVIAN. Lepidus, I trust you have not been waiting long.

LEPIDUS. I was entertained by your charming sister.

OCTAVIAN. Octavia is a creature of the utmost delicacy.

LEPIDUS. Even the most prized piece of porcelain must be taken out of the cupboard occasionally.

OCTAVIAN. Ah, you have been listening to her woeful lamentations.

LEPIDUS. I feel for her distress.

OCTAVIAN. She is young. We will find her a suitable husband in time. And time is what we must discuss. Lepidus, two months, two long months have come and gone and Mark Antony is still in Egypt. Has he brought Cleopatra back in chains? Has he done anything he promised? Yes, he has sailed to Egypt to confront the Queen and now lives there by her side in decadent splendor with no thought of Rome.

LEPIDUS. Who is this poisonous snake who wrecks our men? Caesar first and now Antony. When will it end?

OCTAVIAN. I'll tell you when. Now! This time it's my turn. There will be no more talk of war. There *will* be war! No more shining words but shining steel. Rome will be paved with Antony's blood. And I'll take that Egyptian snake and twist it and twist it and twist it until I ring its tail off!

LEPIDUS. Those are fine words, Octavian, but not for you.

OCTAVIAN. Not for me, Lepidus? You dare insult Octavian!

LEPIDUS. You have the brains and cunning of a great leader but you are missing one important thing. You do not inspire the love of the people.

OCTAVIAN. And I suppose Antony does?

LEPIDUS. One cannot deny that despite his shortcomings, the people adore him.

OCTAVIAN. He is a traitor. A degenerate who lives only for sensual pleasure.

LEPIDUS. That is part of his allure.

OCTAVIAN. The people cannot be so easily swayed.

LEPIDUS. Antony may not be the brightest of fireflies but he fairly glows with virility. When he makes a speech at the Forum, no one is there to listen to the words.

OCTAVIAN. You speak stuff and nonsense.

LEPIDUS. Cast off your ambitions of destroying Antony and place him in your debt.

OCTAVIAN. How do I do that? One can't even persuade the libertine to return to Rome.

LEPIDUS. Write him a letter of contrition.

OCTAVIAN. I'd rather cut off my hand.

LEPIDUS. Write him that you see how blind you were to his unique qualities of leadership. Admit to your own failings. Make him feel that only he can save Rome from civil war.

OCTAVIAN. I agree that Antony is a vain peacock but he is clearly mesmerized by the Egyptian serpent. How do we pry the peacock out of the clutches of the snake?

LEPIDUS. By the lure of another species. Perhaps a delicate songbird. A dewy young virgin next to whom Cleopatra will seem like an old leather saddle.

OCTAVIAN. A dewy young virgin you say? My beauteous twin sister, Octavia, a maiden guileless and pure, pines for marriage. It is too perfect. I shall make a gift of Octavia to Antony. If he is married to my sister, he will be forced to remain in my good graces. That will be the iron chain that will tether the peacock to my throne. If you will forgive me, Sir, I have a most important missive to send to Egypt.

End of Scene

Scene Eight

(Egypt. **IRAS** *and* **CHARMION** *enter with the*
SOOTHSAYER. *The actor playing* **IRAS** *announces*
"Egypt. **CLEOPATRA***'s palace in Alexandria.")*

CHARMION. Soothsayer, I pray that you are here to give Her
Majesty a prophecy of good tidings. She has been so
utterly miserable since Antony has returned to Rome.

SOOTHSAYER. I come here *not* with a prophecy but with
news of Mark Antony. You see, I too have been in
Rome.

IRAS. Blessed Goddess, that is even better than a prophecy.

CHARMION. It's been months since Octavian summoned
Antony to Rome. He was hesitant to leave Cleopatra.
Theirs is a love as precious as a jewel in an Ethiop's ear.
I've never seen her fall for any man like she has for this
one. And oh, the way he loves her. It's a beautiful thing
to see.

SOOTHSAYER. And yet he left her for Rome.

CHARMION. It was the Queen who urged him to go.

IRAS. Cleopatra and Antony can only benefit from an
alliance with Octavian. Alas, she had hoped to receive
regular missives from Antony and thus far has heard
nothing. She fears he may not be well.

SOOTHSAYER. Oh, he's well.

CHARMION. Her Majesty will be most grateful to hear that.

(**CLEOPATRA** *enters.)*

IRAS. Your Majesty, our old friend the Soothsayer has news
for you from Rome.

CLEOPATRA. Are you to bring me comfort? My lord, Mark
Antony, is he well? Does he suffer without me?

(The **SOOTHSAYER** *flings himself to the ground,*
breathless and trembling.)

SOOTHSAYER. Oh, my Queen! My Queen!

CLEOPATRA. What cruel words shall you lay upon my brow?

SOOTHSAYER. Queen, I fear I am the bearer of grievous news.

CLEOPATRA. Antony is dead. Tell me he lives and you shall be rewarded with ropes of the most precious rubies and sapphires.

SOOTHSAYER. Antony is well.

CLEOPATRA. Still you mock me with your grim visage. Speak, before I rip the words from your throat.

SOOTHSAYER. Antony is enjoying great success in Rome. It is said that he has forged a strong alliance with Octavian.

CLEOPATRA. That was my fervent wish. But your air of melancholia makes me fear heartbreak will soon be calling. Antony has promised not to return to Egypt?

SOOTHSAYER. He has made a promise of another kind. To seal the peace he has wooed the noble sister of Octavian.

CLEOPATRA. She is called Octavia. He loves her?

SOOTHSAYER. I only know that he married her.

CLEOPATRA. Married her? Get out! Get out! GET OUT!!!

CHARMION. Mistress!

> (**CLEOPATRA** *puts her foot on the shoulder of the crouching* **SOOTHSAYER**.)

CLEOPATRA. Stay there then – and admit you have lied. If not, those promised ropes of rubies and sapphires will be used as a noose around your neck!

SOOTHSAYER. *(In terror.)* I have told the truth. That is all!

IRAS. Queen, he is an innocent.

CLEOPATRA. He lies!! I shall have my guards sprinkle your body with meat tenderizer and then throw you into a pit full of hungry lions. Married! He is married! He, who swore that only death would sever our passion. Married! While I languish in solitude, asking myself: 'Where is he? Where is he? Where is he?"

CHARMION. Queen, hear me!

CLEOPATRA. Aaaaaaaagh! Antony! He has taken to his marriage bed the sister of our most bitter foe?

CHARMION. Clearly he didn't do it from love.

CLEOPATRA. Charmion, watch what you say.

CHARMION. What he did, he must have had appropriate political reasons for doing it.

CLEOPATRA. *(To the* **SOOTHSAYER.***)* Get up! Get up! Rise! I'm speaking to you!

> *(The* **SOOTHSAYER** *with difficulty rises.)*

SOOTHSAYER. I'm getting too old for this.

CLEOPATRA. *(Desperately trying to control her rage.)* I am no longer angry with you. You did not lie. You are good. You are honest. Tell me, this Octavia – you've seen her?

SOOTHSAYER. Yes, my Queen.

CLEOPATRA. Very close?

SOOTHSAYER. As close as I see you.

CLEOPATRA. Well, what's she like? Tall?

SOOTHSAYER. Moderately so.

CHARMION. I know her seamstress. She's a dwarf.

IRAS. Half my size.

CLEOPATRA. And, you heard her speak? Has she a sweet voice or that of a shrike?

SOOTHSAYER. Quite pleasant.

CHARMION. Pleasant? You've gotta be kidding. Iras, you know her hairdresser.

IRAS. I'm told she squawks like a fishwife.

CLEOPATRA. A fishwife? And her gait? Graceful?

SOOTHSAYER. She is not clumsy.

CHARMION. She's an ox.

IRAS. She walks like she has boulders for buttocks.

> *(***IRAS***,* **CHARMION** *and the* **SOOTHSAYER** *imitate* **OCTAVIA***'s walk.* **CLEOPATRA** *laughs like a child.)*

CLEOPATRA. Look. Is that not an Ibis that brushes the terrace there?

IRAS. Yes, mistress.

CLEOPATRA. This bird has something tied to its wing. Ah, my Apollodorus has captured him.

> (**APOLLODORUS** *enters holding a carrier pigeon.*)

APOLLODORUS. Royal Egypt, this fragile creature had a message for you tied to its delicate wing.

> (*He removes it and hands the message to* **CLEOPATRA.**)

CLEOPATRA. Yes, it's a letter from Antony. Stamped with his seal. To Queen Cleopatra from Carthage. Carthage? "Cleopatra, arm your war fleet and leave for Actium."

CHARMION. Nothing more?

CLEOPATRA. Nothing.

IRAS. What's it mean?

CLEOPATRA. He needs me. And this is my chance to see for myself the boulder-buttocked Octavia. Apollodorus, send the order to the ships at Alexandria to depart.

CHARMION. Shall I pack the wiglets, Your Majesty?

CLEOPATRA. Nah, we can buy new hair in Carthage.

End of Scene

Scene Nine

(Carthage. **ANTONY** *enters and announces "***ANTONY***'s rooms in Carthage."* **OCTAVIA** *joins him.)*

OCTAVIA. What of all these Egyptian ships arriving in the harbor? I'm frightened. What will my brother say?

ANTONY. Octavia, these ships will act as a warning to your brother that Antony is not to be trifled with.

OCTAVIA. I pray that it's only a warning. Do remember that it is thanks to him I am your wife.

ANTONY. Your beloved brother, Octavian, brokered this marriage as a weapon to castrate me and bury me alive as a powerless in-law.

OCTAVIA. I refuse to believe that.

ANTONY. Look at his actions. After Lepidus was deposed, I had a right to my share of his provinces. Your dear twin brother kept everything. He seeks nothing less than to humiliate me.

OCTAVIA. That can't be true. He loves me too much to hurt my husband.

ANTONY. *(Disdainfully.)* My gentle one, you are hopelessly naïve.

OCTAVIA. Do be patient. I beg of you. For me.

ANTONY. It is too late for patience. It is time for force. Armed force.

OCTAVIA. I'm so confused. When I listen to Octavian, it seems to me he's right.

ANTONY. *(Harshly.)* Octavia!

OCTAVIA. But, after you speak – he's in the wrong.

ANTONY. As well he is.

OCTAVIA. Waging war can never be the answer. With my adored husband and my cherished brother waging war on each other, whoever be the victor, I shall be in mourning for the defeated.

ANTONY. Make him recognize his mistakes and there will be peace.

OCTAVIA. I will. I will.

ANTONY. Ah, look, more of the Egyptian fleet is arriving from the South.

OCTAVIA. Antony, please! May I not go to my brother with a compromise?

> (**ANTONY** *exits, followed by a distraught* **OCTAVIA.** *Two young mustached and bearded young men tiptoe into the room wearing short togas. It is* **CHARMION** *and* **IRAS** *in disguise.*)

CHARMION. Well, kid, we got in. I was sure that sentry was on to us.

IRAS. Gee, I don't know how men wear these short skirts. Don't they catch cold?

CHARMION. This must be the master suite. I guess this is as good a place as any to set up shop.

IRAS. Where's the Queen? I hope we didn't lose her.

CHARMION. Your Majesty? Your Majesty!

> (**CLEOPATRA** *enters, also dressed in attractive men's attire, leggings and boots but with a cute short feminine wig and no facial hair. She has kind of a '60s Garland look to her.*)

CLEOPATRA. This is their lodging?

IRAS. Since this morning I am told.

CLEOPATRA. The bed is unmade. They must have spent the night here. I can smell the aftermath of their lovemaking. I can smell their lust. I can smell their deceit.

CHARMION. That's some nose on you. I pray this expedition does not bring you more pain.

IRAS. My prayer is that you will observe a marriage made only out of political need.

CLEOPATRA. *(Motioning to their facial hair.)* Don't you think you two overdid it a bit?

IRAS. We were just being creative.

CLEOPATRA. You both have been acting very strange lately. For months come to think of it.

CHARMION. We were…afraid that our earlier bad humor was causing you undo stress. So we have made a valiant effort to be friends.

IRAS. Most of the time we're faking it. I still can't stand her.

CHARMION. She's a schmuck. That's a new word I just picked up from an Israelite.

CLEOPATRA. *(Suspiciously.)* Uh huh.

CHARMION. Someone's coming. Your Majesty, let us hide behind this arras.

> *(They hide behind a drape.* **ANTONY** *and* **OCTAVIA** *return.)*

OCTAVIA. I suppose you arranged for this fleet through the Queen of Egypt.

ANTONY. Who else?

OCTAVIA. That's what I feared.

ANTONY. Out with it. You think the Queen of Egypt is here in Carthage.

> *(***CLEOPATRA*** and the girls poke their heads out watching them.)*

OCTAVIA. She could very well be. They say she's a witch. Are you under her spell?

ANTONY. You're carrying on like an idiotic servant girl.

OCTAVIA. I believe you are infatuated, madly in love with the serpent of the Nile.

ANTONY. I forbid you to use that vulgar phrase.

> *(***CLEOPATRA*** is thrilled by their marital discord. She pokes the girls in hearty enthusiasm.)*

OCTAVIA. She is a serpent with a long tongue that emits a poison that threatens my marriage.

ANTONY. *(Angry.)* If you were a man, I swear I'd…

> *(He is about to strike her and catches himself.)*

OCTAVIA. Antony, you were about to strike me.

> (CLEOPATRA *is beside herself with joy. Kisses* IRAS *and* CHARMION.)

ANTONY. Forgive me, Octavia. I'm afraid my blood is simmering for battle.

OCTAVIA. In my own way, I too am prepared for battle – against Cleopatra.

> (CLEOPATRA *rolls her eyes and silently laughs at that ridiculous notion. "Her?"*)

ANTONY. I command you as your husband to put such thoughts out of your mind.

OCTAVIA. There are times when we are alone, even in our lovemaking, when I feel her baleful eyes upon us. She is here with us now!

> (OCTAVIA *means that metaphorically but* CLEOPATRA *quickly hides behind the curtain.*)

ANTONY. You have no reason to be jealous. Your radiant youth, your delicate beauty; they are gifts the Queen of Egypt can only dream of.

> (CLEOPATRA *pokes her head out again alone, this time wondering what the hell is going on.*)

ANTONY. Let her come and compare herself to you!

OCTAVIA. Tell me you never really loved her.

ANTONY. Love her? Don't make me laugh. I endured making love to her only out of blinding ambition.

> (CLEOPATRA, *in a titanic rage, furiously gives them both the finger. The two girls join her.*)

ANTONY. And it's served me well. I am back in Rome in a position of power, and with the aging lovestruck Egyptian Queen at my beck and call.

> (CLEOPATRA *makes a silent scream.*)

OCTAVIA. Oh, how I worship you. Your ardent passion has brought me to a pitch of erotic fervor. How I long for night to fall and to be once more your banquet to devour.

ANTONY. Appetizer, entrée and dessert.

OCTAVIA. Oh, and what you've done to my *amuse bouche.*

> (CLEOPATRA *falls back behind the curtain as if fainting, followed by her girls.*)

OCTAVIA. My lord, you have taught me that submission is not defeat, but its own form of power. Take me here. Now. Plunder me. I demand it. Do I shock you with my perversity?

ANTONY. Kinda.

OCTAVIA. I long to feel your glorious manhood held taut within my womanly grippers.

ANTONY. *(Seductively.)* Patience, Octavia, patience.

OCTAVIA. *(Lasciviously.)* You motherfucker.

> (CLEOPATRA *and her girls once more peek out from behind the curtain.* CLEOPATRA *is beside herself.*)

ANTONY. My lustful beauty, to think that you should be jealous of that grotesque old slag with her sagging pendulous udders and stretched out greying pudenda. *(He roars with laughter.)*

OCTAVIA. *(Giggling.)* You mustn't. Now you are making me feel pity for the sad old Queen.

> (CLEOPATRA *grabs* IRAS *by the throat and begins strangling her.* CHARMION *pulls the curtain shut.*)

ANTONY. Ah, your compassion is boundless.

OCTAVIA. I will find Octavian. I will implore him to be fair to you and give you what you feel is your due.

ANTONY. Go to him now, my precious one.

> (*She exits.* ANTONY *smirks arrogantly at his handling of the women in his life. The curtain suddenly parts and* CLEOPATRA *reveals herself. The girls have vanished.*)

CLEOPATRA. My eyes and ears burn with bitter truths.

ANTONY. What truth do you speak of?

CLEOPATRA. The unhappy truth that Cleopatra has been betrayed.

ANTONY. Anything you may have overheard was a part of a greater political stratagem.

CLEOPATRA. You might fool a pathetic virgin with that excuse but not this "grotesque old slag."

ANTONY. She is Octavian's sister! I must assure her that you are nothing to me.

CLEOPATRA. Well, you were most convincing. Here I sail for so many days and nights upon your command, and this, this is what I'm greeted with.

ANTONY. My wish was to be joined by the Queen of Egypt, not some harpy in ridiculous male drag.

CLEOPATRA. A harpy. More insults.

ANTONY. Your mad jealousy has turned you into a monster.

CLEOPATRA. No, it is you who turned a loving queen into a monster through your cruelty.

ANTONY. Play the martyr but perhaps I am the one who has cause to be jealous.

CLEOPATRA. What the hell are you talking about?

ANTONY. Don't think I haven't heard foul rumors of your erotic calisthenics with any number of musclebound servants.

CLEOPATRA. Who spreads this poison? Octavian. Antony, listen to us. We are falling right into Octavian's trap.

ANTONY. Yes. This was his master plan for us to destroy each other. And he knows that part of me does hate you.

CLEOPATRA. You hate me?

(He takes her in his arms.)

ANTONY. Yes, I hate you, my sorceress. Away from you, I could breathe. I thought myself free from our fatal love. But there you are. I am hopelessly bewitched.

CLEOPATRA. Watch what you say. Octavia may be in the next room.

ANTONY. Never mind that child who was sold to one who shall always belong to another. You are my vision, my heart, my strength.

CLEOPATRA. You cannot have us both.

ANTONY. You, you alone and always you.

CLEOPATRA. Our alliance shall be viewed by Octavian as an act of war.

ANTONY. Then we go to war!

CLEOPATRA. Antony, allow Cleopatra the jubilation of lighting the first torch of battle.

ANTONY. Yes! You shall set the torch aflame! Glory to Mark Antony and Cleopatra!

CLEOPATRA. To Victory! To Cleopatra and Mark Antony! And to our love!

End of Scene

Scene Ten

(IRAS, CHARMION, APOLLODORUS and the SOOTHSAYER enter. APOLLODORUS announces "CLEOPATRA's ship off the coast of Actium." The light is a flickering red from the flames of battle. The four of them stand by the railing watching the Egyptian fleet go down.)

IRAS. The sea is full of death. Dead soldiers floating to the afterworld.

CHARMION. The battle is so near. I can smell the burning oil. Is Antony still out there?

SOOTHSAYER. He will not accept defeat. His ships are in flames.

IRAS. What went wrong?

APOLLODORUS. Antony's insurrection was doomed from the start. None of his generals or troops would rally to him. They refused to fight against Rome. He had to make due with an untrained Egyptian fleet. What ensued was a bloodbath.

SOOTHSAYER. I saw the whole thing coming.

CHARMION. Poor Antony. Poor Queen.

IRAS. Hey, let me look at your arm.

(CHARMION lifts her arm.)

CHARMION. Yeah?

IRAS. Where'd you get that bangle?

CHARMION. From a tradesman on the street. Pretty, isn't it?

IRAS. That's no ordinary bangle. It's from the temple of Anubis.

CHARMION. Well, I don't know how he got a hold of it.

IRAS. The only one who has possession of that kind of bracelet is the temple's resident vestal virgin. If I recall a week ago you and I met that virgin at the Luxor Baths.

CHARMION. Where are you going with this?

SOOTHSAYER. It's most improper to discuss anything of a personal nature at this tragic moment.

IRAS. You saw her again, didn't you? And she gave you that bracelet.

CHARMION. I forgot. I guess she did. She's a nice girl.

IRAS. I bet she's real nice.

CHARMION. Iras, let's not get into this in front of all these people.

APOLLODORUS. What's going on between you two?

CHARMION. Nothing. She's got the rag on.

IRAS. Let 'em know that you've been cheating on me.

CHARMION. You and your jealousy. The girl's a vestal virgin.

IRAS. That fucked out blonde's had more things in her than King Tut's tomb. I've sacrificed everything for you. I've given you my youth.

CHARMION. And I'm tired of hearing about it.

IRAS. Take off that bracelet or I'll rip it off you.

CHARMION. Go ahead and try.

> *(Once again, the two girls start cat fighting.* **APOLLODORUS** *tries to tear them apart.)*

SOOTHSAYER. Lesbians! Lesbians, please stop!

> *(The two girls suddenly realize their foolishness and begin kissing passionately.)*

IRAS. My darling, how foolish I am to be jealous. I just love you so.

CHARMION. I was seething with jealousy over you and that Nubian slave girl, merely because I found a wiry black hair at the corner of your mouth.

APOLLODORUS. *(Pleased for them.)* So you two are like… together?

CHARMION & **IRAS.** *(Sheepishly.)* Yeah.

SOOTHSAYER. I do not condemn you, for nature has made you this way. But shame on you both for causing such a ruckus on this ship. Here when our Queen is so distraught over her Antony's fate.

APOLLODORUS. All this needless chatter. You'd think we were stalling for time because someone was making a costume change.

(CLEOPATRA enters with great determination.)

CLEOPATRA. Doris! Day will soon be with us.

APOLLODORUS. Mistress, I must inform you that all is lost. Your fleet has been vanquished.

CLEOPATRA. But I am told Antony lives! He must be rescued off of his burning ship.

CHARMION. How is that possible?

CLEOPATRA. I have arranged for a small sailing vessel, a felucca, to take me to him. I am ready to depart. We will sail to the Upper Nile and disappear among the tall reeds.

IRAS. And then what?

CLEOPATRA. We will find some place where we can lose ourselves, have each other to love and still be happy.

SOOTHSAYER. I see no future in this plan.

CLEOPATRA. A different future. I am prepared to give up my throne to Octavian if I must.

IRAS. This is madness! Can't someone talk sense into her?

(CAESAR's ghost appears. No one but CLEOPATRA can see him.)

CAESAR. Cleopatra!

CLEOPATRA. I knew you would come.

CAESAR. I promised to guide you when you arrived at a crossroad.

CHARMION. Who is she speaking to?

SOOTHSAYER. I believe it to be great Caesar's shade.

CLEOPATRA. Can you see him as well?

SOOTHSAYER. *(Fiddling with his ear for clarity.)* Just the audio.

CAESAR. If you never again listen to any words of council, then listen to me now. Dismiss any lunatic idea of rescuing Antony.

CLEOPATRA. You cannot demand this of me. I love him.

CAESAR. Antony is a soldier. He lives by a code of honor. To flee from his men in defeat is to be branded forever a coward. If you force him to be less of himself, he will despise you for the rest of his days.

CLEOPATRA. He will never despise me. We are one beating heart. I cannot let him die.

CHARMION. But mistress, you both may die in this mad escape.

IRAS. Please, I beg of you don't do this.

SOOTHSAYER. You must not give up your throne.

APOLLODORUS. Antony would prefer death to disgrace.

CAESAR. Don't make this decision for him.

(All of their next lines overlap.)

CHARMION. Please don't! I beg of you. Don't!

IRAS. Don't leave us. Please!

SOOTHSAYER. Don't be hasty. Don't be rash.

APOLLODORUS. Don't make Antony less of a man.

CAESAR. You must listen to reason. Don't be a fool!

CLEOPATRA. Don't! Don't! Don't tell me not to sail I've simply got to! I care not for any danger that might befall me. Only that I must forge onward, ever onward, to my destiny and to my love. *(She exits.)*

End of Scene

Scene Eleven

(CLEOPATRA's tomb in Alexandria. CLEOPATRA and CAESAR have remained in place from the previous scene. The actor playing CAESAR announces "Alexandria, the tomb of CLEOPATRA." He exits. The mortally wounded ANTONY is helped on by APOLLODORUS. He lays ANTONY down on a platform. CLEOPATRA crosses to him and cradles his head in her arms.)

ANTONY. I am dying, Egypt. I am dying.

CLEOPATRA. You must use my love to bind your wounds.

ANTONY. How deep does a man have to stab himself to die? Why? Why did you take me from battle?

CLEOPATRA. I could not live without you. Why did you plunge that knife into your flesh?

ANTONY. I could not live without honor. But future generations will envy me because I died in your arms. One more kiss, Cleopatra.

(She kisses him. He dies. APOLLODORUS lifts the dead ANTONY is his arms and carries him off stage. None of this is played for comic effect. For this moment, we have moved into tragedy.)

CLEOPATRA. Noblest of men, shall I abide in this dull world alone, which in thy absence is no better than a sty?

(A fanfare is heard. OCTAVIAN, every bit the Emperor and in full Imperial battle regalia, enters.)

OCTAVIAN. Cleopatra!

CLEOPATRA. I should have expected you. The victor.

OCTAVIAN. Yes, the victor. I chose conquest over passion. That, Royal Egypt, was your downfall. You stare at me with your cat eyes. What do you see before you?

CLEOPATRA. I see that despite your golden armor you are still a boy. You will always be a boy.

OCTAVIAN. Well, the boy has brought the great Antony to his doom. The boy has taken claim of your throne, your lands, your kingdom. They are all the spoils of war. However, I am not heartless. I will permit you to rule Egypt as a Roman province under one condition.

CLEOPATRA. You wish me to return with you to Rome and be paraded through the Forum behind your chariot in chains.

OCTAVIAN. I do not wish it. I demand it. Your humiliation will teach others the folly of waging war on Rome. After this display, you shall be returned to Egypt. Where is your son? I should have thought he'd be by your side in this time of trial.

CLEOPATRA. He is blessedly far from here. If I go with you to Rome will you allow my son to rule Egypt and his sons and theirs?

OCTAVIAN. I do not see why not.

CLEOPATRA. Do I have your word as a Roman Emperor… and a God?

OCTAVIAN. Absolutely. *(Behind his back, we see he has his fingers crossed.)*

CLEOPATRA. If you would leave now, I shall prepare for my journey.

OCTAVIAN. Do I have your word that you will not harm yourself in any way?

CLEOPATRA. Absolutely.

> *(OCTAVIAN cannot see that behind her back, her fingers are also crossed.)*

OCTAVIAN. I shall hold you to that. My men will be back shortly.

> *(OCTAVIAN turns and leaves. CHARMION and IRAS approach her.)*

IRAS. Let me die before I see you go to Rome in chains. Defeated.

CHARMION. I too am content to die with you.

CLEOPATRA. Girls, I'm not going to Rome. I never intended to.

> *(**APOLLODORUS** enters carrying a small basket.)*

APOLLODORUS. All is as you requested, Sovereign.

CLEOPATRA. Doris, you have always served me well.

APOLLODORUS. I thank thee, my Queen. And with my dagger plunged deeply into my heart, I shall accompany my sovereign on her final voyage.

> *(**CLEOPATRA** opens the basket and removes a small snake, the asp. She holds it to her breast.)*

CLEOPATRA. Ah, you pretty reptile, wake up. Don't keep me waiting, darling.

IRAS. *(Crying.)* Oh, Mistress!

CLEOPATRA. Charming asp, make of me your meal. I have immortal longings in me.

> *(**CLEOPATRA** is bitten. She returns the snake to the basket. **APOLLODORUS** and the girls kneel at her feet.)*

Iras, give me my mirror so I can see if I remain beautiful while dying.

> *(**IRAS** gives her a small hand mirror. The Queen regards herself objectively.)*

Not bad. All things considered. *(She returns the mirror to **IRAS**. The two girls weep.)* Girls, look well for love. Look well. And if you are fortunate to find it, give all. And now, my precious ones, I look forward to beginning my voyage to the afterworld.

CHARMION. Mistress, your tomb will be prepared for your every need. Shall I pack the wiglets?

CLEOPATRA. Nah, we can pick up new hair in—Yes, dear Charmion, pack the wiglets.

> *(**CLEOPATRA** dies in a beautiful tableau with her three devoted servants at her feet. The music swells.)*

End of Play